This house, once

This house, once

DEBORAH FREEDMAN

A
atheneum

Atheneum Books for Young Readers

New York   London   Toronto   Sydney   New Delhi

ATHENEUM BOOKS FOR YOUNG READERS
An imprint of Simon & Schuster Children's Publishing Division
1230 Avenue of the Americas, New York, New York 10020
Copyright © 2017 by Deborah Freedman
ATHENEUM BOOKS FOR YOUNG READERS is a registered trademark of Simon & Schuster, Inc.
Atheneum logo is a trademark of Simon & Schuster, Inc.
For information about special discounts for bulk purchases, please contact Simon & Schuster Special Sales
at 1-866-506-1949 or business@simonandschuster.com.
The Simon & Schuster Speakers Bureau can bring authors to your live event. For more information or to
book an event, contact the Simon & Schuster Speakers Bureau at 1-866-248-3049 or visit our website at
www.simonspeakers.com.
Book design by Ann Bobco
The text for this book was set in pencilPete FONT.
The illustrations for this book were rendered in pencil, watercolor, and bits of colored pencil and pan
pastel, with an assist from Photoshop.
Manufactured in China
1016 SCP
First Edition
10 9 8 7 6 5 4 3 2 1
Library of Congress Cataloging-in-Publication Data
Freedman, Deborah (Deborah Jane), 1960- author, illustrator.
This house, once / Deborah Freedman. — First edition.
pages cm
Summary: Asks readers to think about ways in which the natural world has provided for them, by exploring
all the different elements of a house and where each came from, once.
ISBN 978-1-4814-4284-8 (hardcover)
ISBN 978-1-4814-4285-5 (eBook)
[1. Dwellings—Fiction. 2. Nature—Fiction.] I. Title.
PZ7.F87276Th 2017
[E]—dc23   2015011937

This book is for Emma—

who with Lucie and Ben made our house a home.

This door was once a colossal oak tree
about three hugs around
and as high as the blue.

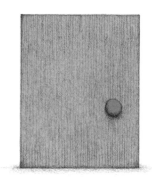

These stones were once below,
underground, deep asleep,
tucked beneath
a blanket of leaves.

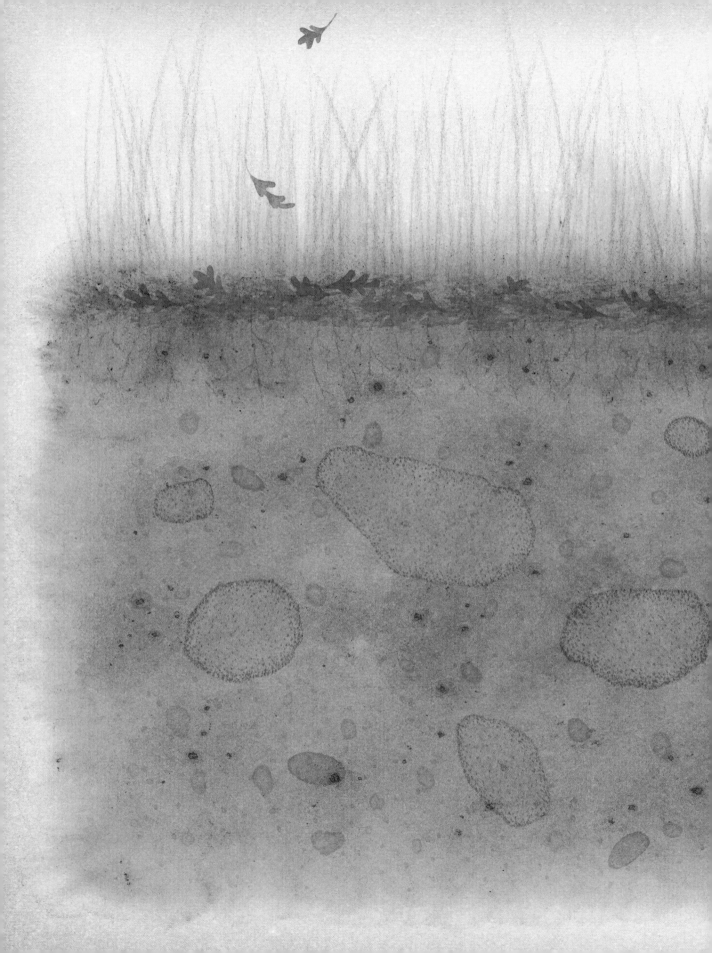

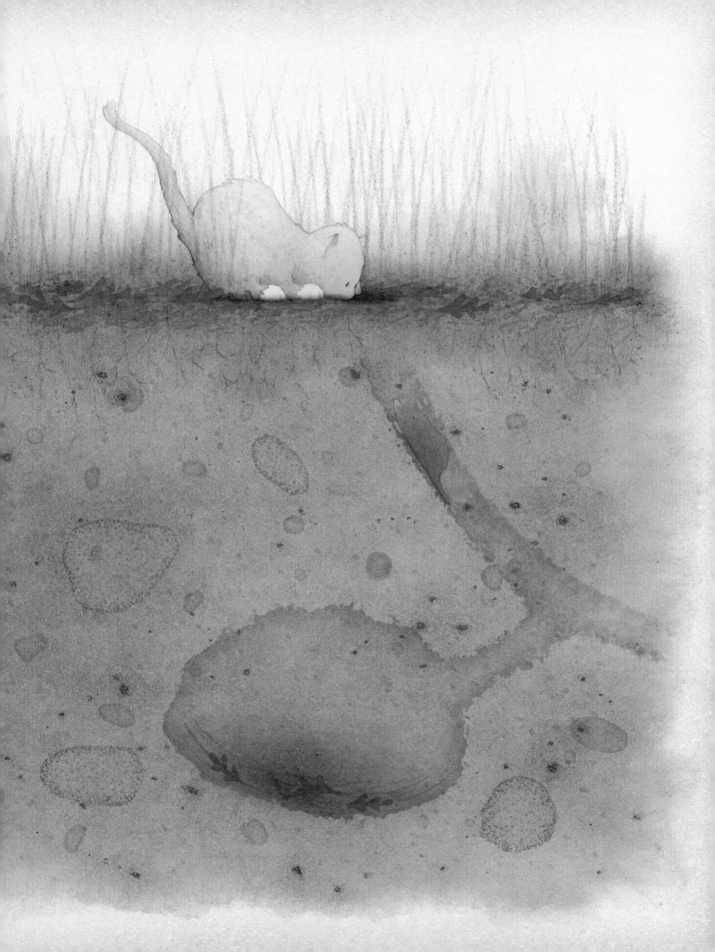

These bricks were once mud
that oozed around roots,
sticky and loose
before formed and baked hard.

This roof was once rock,
carved and cleft

and shingled to shelter

from gray wet

and cold.

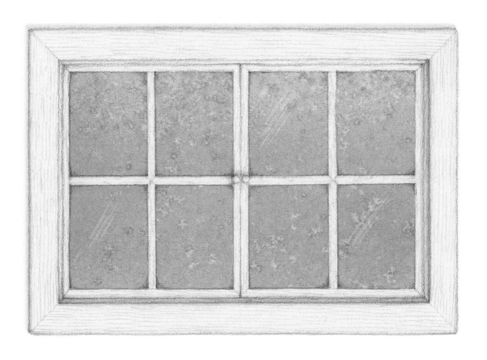

This window was sand once,

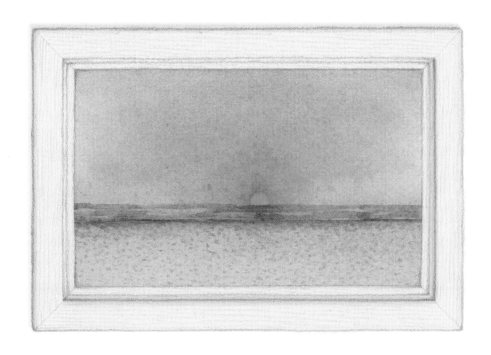

that melted to glass

in flames, like the fire

that warms this house

and lights doorknob, bookshelf,

under-the-stair . . .

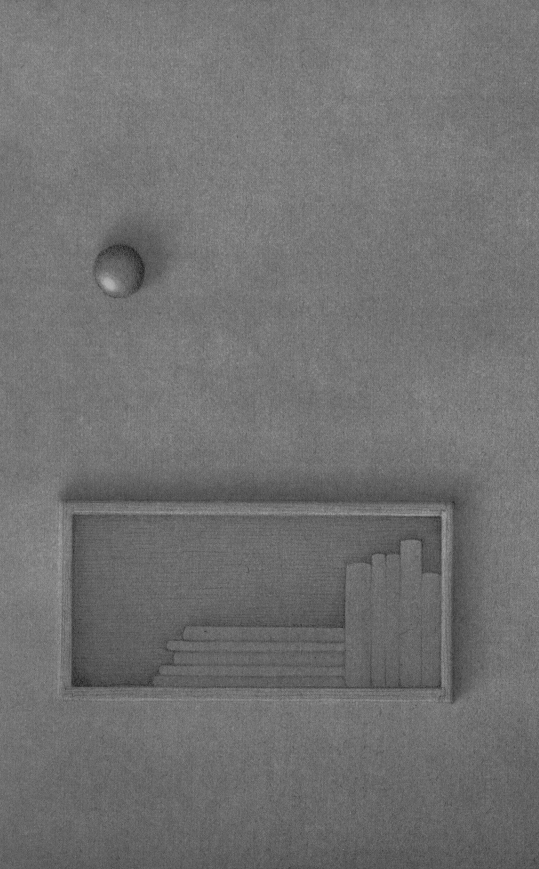

What were these all, once?

This house remembers,

drowsy with dreams

that drift in through this door,

which once

was an oak.

NOTE TO READERS

I live in New England, in a house built on rocky earth and a base made of brick, with a strong oak door, and a slate roof that shrugs off rain and soaks up sun.

Where do *you* live? What was *your* home, once?

ACKNOWLEDGMENTS

Many, many thanks to Stephen Barr and to everyone at Atheneum—especially Ann Bobco and Emma Ledbetter.

7/18